espresso
education

Phonics

Gym
Club

KU-114-797

Gill Budgell

W
FRANKLIN WATTS
LONDON•SYDNEY

First published in 2012 by
Franklin Watts
338 Euston Road
London NW1 3BH

Franklin Watts Australia
Level 17/207 Kent Street
Sydney NSW 2000

Text and illustration © Franklin Watts 2012

The Espresso characters are originated and
designed by Claire Underwood and Pesky Ltd.

The Espresso characters are the property of
Espresso Education Ltd.

A CIP catalogue record for this book is
available from the British Library.

ISBN: 978 1 4451 0754 7 (hbk)
ISBN: 978 1 4451 0757 8 (pbk)

Illustrations by Artful Doodlers Ltd.
Art Director: Jonathan Hair
Series Editor: Jackie Hamley
Project Manager: Gill Budgell
Series Designer: Matthew Lilly

Printed in China

Franklin Watts is a division of
Hachette Children's Books,
an Hachette UK company.

www.hachette.co.uk

Level 1 50 words
Concentrating on CVC words plus and, the, to

Level 2 70 words
Concentrating on double letter sounds and new letter
sounds (ck, ff, ll, ss, j, v, w, x, y, z, zz) plus no, go, I

Level 3 100 words
Concentrating on new graphemes (qu, ch, sh, th, ng,
ai, ee, igh, oa, oo, ar, or, ur, ow, oi, ear, air, ure, er)
plus he, she, we, me, be, was, my, you, they, her, all

Level 4 150 words
Concentrating on adjacent consonants (CVCC/CCVC
words) plus said, so, have, like, some, come, were, there,
little, one, do, when, out, what

Level 5 180 words
Concentrating on new graphemes (ay, wh, ue, ir, ou, aw,
ph, ew, ea, a-e, e-e, i-e, o-e, u-e) plus day, very, put, time,
about, saw, here, came, made, don't, asked, looked,
called, Mrs

Level 6 200 words
Concentrating on alternative pronunciations (c, ow, o, g, y)
and spellings (ee, ur, ay, or, m, n, air, l, r) plus your, don't
time, saw, here, very, make, their, called, asked, looked

Polly and Sal were fed up.
"There must be somewhere
to go," said Polly.
"Let's go to the Crystal Gym,"
said Sal.

"I don't know what to do at the gym," said Polly.

"It isn't scary. Just copy me," Sal said.

At the gym they had to sign in.
"Write your name there and tear
off that bit," said Sal.

Then they went to put on their kit.

Rob from the gym
took them round.

"There's no mystery but you need to take care," he said.

"On this you must push and pull,"
Rob said.
Sal did it well.

Polly did it wrong and
hurt her thumb.

"Climb up and down like this,"
Rob said.
Sal did it well.

Polly did it wrong and
hurt her knee.

"You go first," said Sal.
But Polly did it wrong.

"Take care. No need to wrench it!" Rob said to Polly.

"You will be a wreck
at this rate," said Sal.
They took a rest.

"Let's get a pear drink
to share," said Sal.

"I will get it. You grab a chair," Polly said.

As Sal got on
the chair …

Over it went!

Crash!

"You didn't do that very well!" said Polly.

Puzzle Time

Match the words to the picture if they have the same sound in them. One has been done for you.

Look out! They might be different spellings for the same sound.

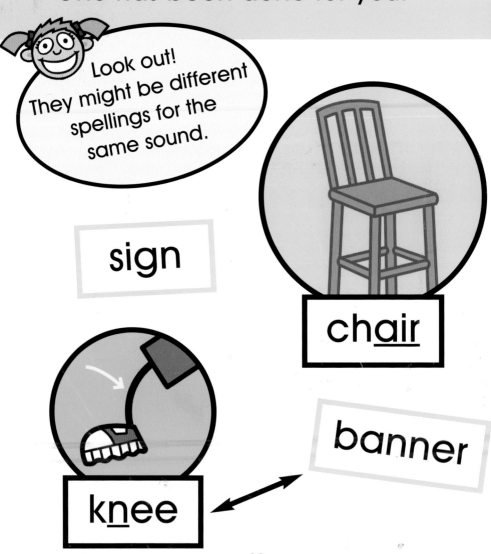

sign

chair

knee

banner

22

care

wrong

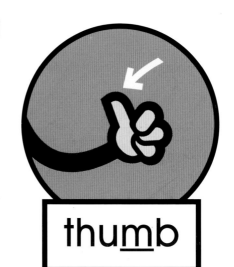

thu__m__b

climb

hammer

pear

arrow

w__r__ite

Answers

knee – banner is already completed to show how the same sound **/n/** but different letters **kn** and **nn** can make a pair.

knee /n/ – banner, sign   **thumb /m/** – hammer, climb
chair /air/ – care, pear   **write /r/** – arrow, wrong

A note about the phonics in this book

Alternative spellings of known phonemes

Known phonemes	New graphemes/spellings	Words in the story
/m/	/m/ as mb	thumb, climb
/n/	/n/ as gn, kn	knee, know, sign
/air/	/air/ as ere, ear, are, eir	somewhere, scary, care, tear, there, their, pear, share, chair
/i/	/i/ as y	crystal, gym, mystery
/r/	/r/ as wr	write, wreck, wrench, wrong
common words	your, don't	
tricky common words	their	

Remind children about the letters they already know for these phonemes.

In the puzzle they are challenged to match the words to the picture if they have the same sound in them; the same sound but different letters.

Top tip: if a child gets stuck on a word then ask them to try and sound it out and then blend it together again or show them how to do this. For example, crystal, c-r-i-s-t-(a)l, crystal.